Disney BOOKS BY MAIL

Produced by The Creative Spark
San Clemente, California

Illustrated by Yakovetic Productions

Printed in the United States of America.

ISBN 1-56326-158-8

Scuttle's Last
Flight

It's too bad my friends can't fly, Scuttle thought as he floated high above the clouds. *They'd love the view from up here.*

The warm summer wind lifted the seagull higher and higher until he neared the top of the island. The wind whooshed across his feathers, making him feel as fast and sleek as an eagle. Of course, he wasn't an eagle, he was a seagull – and he wasn't looking where he was going.

"Be careful, Scuttle!" Ariel cried out from below, but it was too late. The bird crashed right into the side of the mountain!

The next thing Scuttle knew, he was flat on his back in front of the cave where Scales the dragon lived. Ariel, Scales, and Sebastian all rushed to his side. "We tried to warn you," the Little Mermaid said, "but I guess you didn't hear us. Are you all right?"

"I don't know," the woozy bird replied. "I think I hurt my wing."

While Scales and Sebastian helped their friend get back on his feet, Ariel made a sling of seaweed for his injured wing. "There you go," she said as she slipped the sling on Scuttle. "I'm sure you'll be good as new in no time."

But a week later, Scuttle was still wearing his sling. He hadn't flown a single time since the accident! "I'm worried about Scuttle," Ariel confided to Sebastian. "His wing doesn't seem to be getting any better."

Sebastian wasn't so sure. He thought Scuttle might be pretending. "Why would he do a thing like that?" Ariel asked.

"Because he's afraid to fly again," the clever crab said.

That night, Sebastian followed Scuttle and watched as the bird used his injured wing to get pickles – his favorite food – out of a pickle jar. His wing had healed after all!

There's nothing wrong with his wing, Sebastian thought. *It's his confidence that needs fixing.*

The next morning, Sebastian told Ariel and Scales what he had seen.
"We've got to find a way to make Scuttle fly again," Scales said. "He's
afraid to try it on his own."

Ariel had an idea. "I bet I know how to make him fly again,"
she said.

Just then Scuttle came walking down the beach. "Hi, everybody!" he said to his friends, but Ariel just sighed. "Is something wrong?" the bird asked.

"See those beautiful flowers?" Ariel said, pointing to the hibiscus that grew on a nearby hillside. "I want to wear a flower in my hair, but I can't reach them from here."

"I'll get you a flower for your hair!" Scuttle said.

"You will?" replied the Little Mermaid hopefully. She was sure her plan had worked. But instead of flying to the hillside, Scuttle simply plucked a water lily from the lagoon. "Here you are," he said as he presented it to Ariel. "A beautiful flower for a beautiful mermaid."

"So much for that plan," Sebastian whispered to Scales.

The next day, Sebastian set up his easel and started to paint. He had the perfect plan to get Scuttle flying again.

"That's a very pretty picture," Scuttle said, looking over Sebastian's shoulder.

"Why, thank you," the crab replied, "but it needs something else. I know! It needs a bird flying across the sky. I wonder who I could get to pose for me."

Sebastian was sure his friend would fly now, because Scuttle loved to have his picture painted. Instead, Scuttle just pointed to a pelican flying overhead. "Look! There goes a bird now!" he said triumphantly.

Later, Sebastian told Scales about how his plan had failed.

"I know!" Scales said to Sebastian. "If we could get you to the top of that tree, then Scuttle would have to fly up to save you!"

"How would we do that?" Sebastian asked nervously.

"Like this!" the dragon replied, and before Sebastian could stop him, Scales tossed his friend high into the air.

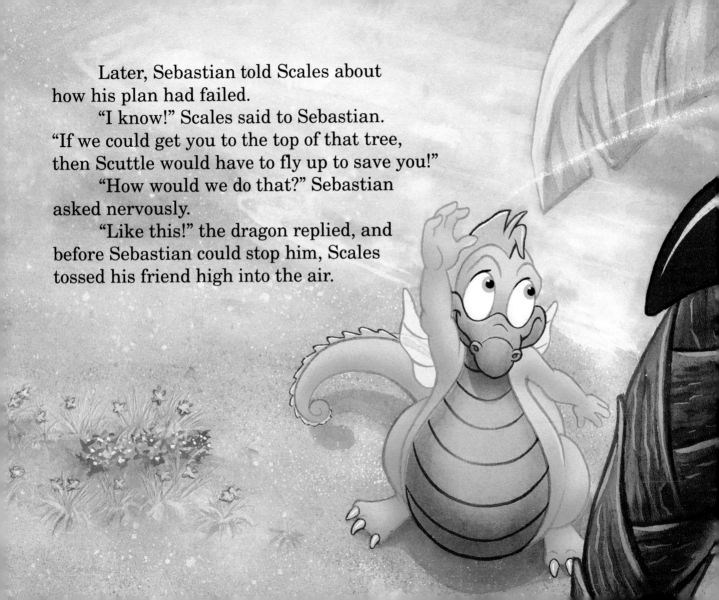

"Help! Get me down from here!" Sebastian cried. "It's too high!"
"That's good!" Scales called out. "Keep pretending you're scared while I hide."
"Who's pretending?" the crab screeched.

Just then Scuttle waddled by. "Help, Scuttle!" Sebastian called out.
"Get me down from here!"

"Sure thing!" Scuttle called back. He started rocking the tree.

"What are you doing?" cried Sebastian.

"I'm getting you out of the tree!" Scuttle said, as Sebastian sailed out
into the lagoon and landed with a big SPLASH!

"You ought to be more careful," Scuttle said as Sebastian swam back to shore. "How did you get stuck in that tree anyway?"

"I did it on purpose so you'd have to fly up and save me!" Sebastian said, losing his temper. "Don't you see? We've all been trying to get you to fly! Your wing isn't hurt anymore—you've just lost confidence in yourself. If you really wanted to, you could fly again."

Later, as Scuttle finished the last of his pickles, he thought about what Sebastian had said. *Maybe they're right,* he thought to himself. *Maybe I am afraid to fly.*

Just then, Scuttle saw a ship sailing by in the distance. It was the S.S. Pickle! *Hmm*, the hungry bird thought. *If Sebastian is right, then I could just fly out there and take a look.*

Scuttle took a deep breath. He stretched out his wings. Could he really do it? Could he still fly?

Scuttle took off the sling. He flapped his wings as hard as he could. At first, nothing happened, but then, very slowly, he felt his feet lifting off the ground. He was flying!

Now Scuttle understood why his friends had tried to help him. *They knew all I needed to fly again was a little confidence,* he thought as he glided out to the ship.

And Scuttle was rewarded for his flight, too. There, bobbing in the ocean below, was a great big jar of pickles that had fallen overboard.

Scuttle scooped up the jar and turned back. He circled the island, calling out to his friends below, "Hey! Look at me! I'm flying again!"

"Pickles!" Sebastian said to Ariel. "Why didn't we think of pickles?"

"The important thing is, Scuttle has his confidence back," Ariel replied.

It was true. Scuttle was his old self again, sailing high above the clouds. *I wish my friends could fly, too,* Scuttle thought as the wind whooshed across his feathers. *They'd love the view from up here!*